LOVING HER
UNLEASHING HELL BOOK TWO

VIOLA TEMPEST

Loving Her
Unleashing Hell Book Two

© Copyright 2022 Viola Tempest

All rights reserved. No part of this publication may be reproduced, distributed, or transmitted in any form or by any means, including photocopying, recording, or other electronic or mechanical methods, without the prior written permission of the publisher, except in the case of brief quotations embodied in critical reviews and certain other non-commercial uses permitted by copyright law.
Any references to historical events, real people, or real places are used fictitiously. Names, characters, and places are products of the author's imagination.

Cover Design by Burning Phoenix Covers

CONTENTS

Chapter 1	1
Chapter 2	11
Chapter 3	31
Chapter 4	47
Chapter 5	61
Chapter 6	71
Chapter 7	87

UNLEASHING HELL BOOK TWO

LOVING HER

VIOLA TEMPEST

CHAPTER 1

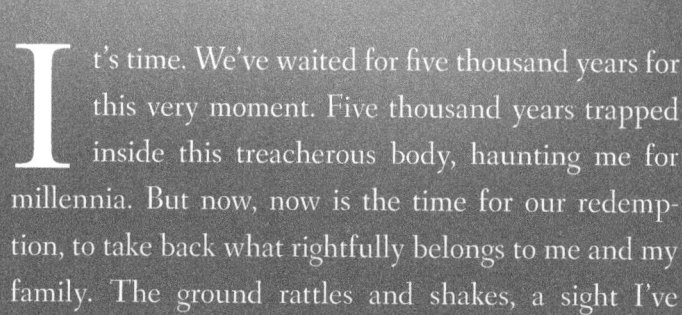

It's time. We've waited for five thousand years for this very moment. Five thousand years trapped inside this treacherous body, haunting me for millennia. But now, now is the time for our redemption, to take back what rightfully belongs to me and my family. The ground rattles and shakes, a sight I've longed for, for more years than I dare to count.

It's time for the humans to suffer like we have. I

walk closer to the surface of the Earth, listening to their mundane conversations above me, and I chuckle. That light vibration, barely a quiver in the grand scheme of things, and they're already whimpering like the dogs they are. All that money, all that pride and pretense, I'm surprised the little earthquake hasn't sent them running for their rockets to jet off toward the stars in fear.

I don't hate humans, not entirely. They're an ignorant breed, but I can't hate them when I was once *one* of them, walking through life as oblivious to the universe as they are. If I hadn't fallen to the tragedy of living in the Underworld, I would never have come to the realization that it's important not to make enemies of others.

I've spent centuries regretting my actions. Why had I been so rash? Why didn't I just keep my opinions to myself? If I had, none of us would be in this mess. I ruined my life, and the lives of my family; they're paying the price for my mistakes. I was young, I was impetuous, but they were persecuting *us* because we were different. Didn't that mean *anything* to them?

Of course, I was going to defend my people; of course, I was going to scream bloody murder. Should I have known better? Yeah, of course, I should have. I didn't help my family in the slightest; I only made things a hundred times worse than they already were.

I proved those ignorant human fools right; I proved their point... but could they have maybe had a little compassion for us as well? Was that too much to ask?

"Charlie! Grab the keys! Grabs the beans and the chicken! It's happening! The apocalypse is nigh!" I hear an elderly woman shout above my head.

"Goodness, Betsy, how many goddamn times have I told you? It's not an apocalypse; it's just a little earthquake!" The elderly man, Charlie, replies.

"Whatever it is, I'm not about to stand up here and risk it. We need to get to the bomb shelter. Did you go to the Nova's? Are they coming?"

"I tried knocking on their door, but no one answered. Come on, before it gets any worse."

"I thought you said it was just a 'little' earthquake?!" Betsy snaps back, their voices growing dim as they move away from where I stand.

I chuckle. Just a little earthquake. I can understand why they might think that. I mean, who *really* expects the beginning of the end? Their innocence is amusing to me. Betsy's right, though. She's one of the few lunatics who actually aren't as crazy as the world thinks they are.

If only they really knew what happened every thousand years; if only they remembered or even believed the stories their ancestors left behind for them. If only they knew; if only they *believed* that every thousand years, the ground reopens, and the creatures of the Underworld travel to the surface to reclaim what had once been theirs. The ultimate battle between two species, where neither side is guaranteed safety. Maybe if they knew, they would be more forgiving... or at least, more repenting.

Anyone who wants to become immortal doesn't know anything about living forever. Life becomes monotonous, meaningless, when they're forced to relive the same events over and over again with no end. Always the same outcome, always the same result, because no one ever learns. A perpetual cycle, an endless loop.

I used to lie awake at night and wonder about the creatures living outside the realm of Earth, wondering what the species living in other dimensions live like. Wishing, dreaming, that I were one of them, something *other* than human. They always say be careful what you wish for, and they're right. Because now, I'm living that life, and I have regretted it ever since.

My mother always told me not to be afraid, that the creatures I felt wanted to hurt me might actually have something else going on, and might actually need help themselves. A bit like bullies. Sometimes, people hurt others because they're being hurt themselves, and it's their way of dealing with what they're going through.

I didn't believe her; what kid would? I shunned the

idea, as all humans do, refusing to trust anyone or anything that might hurt me. I guess this is karma, giving me a taste of my own medicine.

I stand guard, holding my ground as the layer above me continues to shake. The black ground beneath my feet feels softer than usual, like stepping into wet or loose soil, threatening to suck me down into it and never let me go. Never, in the five thousand years of my life down here, have I ever experienced this. I don't remember it *ever* feeling this way, and it strikes me as odd, but I have bigger things to deal with — much more important things. Like my freedom.

I have a mission, and I owe it to my family not to get distracted by something as trivial as the *ground* feeling weird. It's probably nothing, after all.

"Get ready!" I call over my shoulder to my family as they stand behind me, holding hands, alongside other members of our coven.

Any minute now. Any minute, and the ground above us will crack open and reveal the world above our heads, always just out of reach, until now. The doorway to our freedom.

This isn't the first time the door has revealed itself to us; in fact, it's the fourth time that I can recall. Unfortunately, as life would have it, none of the previous times have been successful. Climbing onto the surface and taking back what's rightfully ours isn't as simple as killing a few humans to regain control. Even if we prove victorious, despite many fallen victims, the curse they put on us forces us to remain in these wretched bodies. Without the amulet and the power of the Chosen One, *nothing* we do will ever give us salvation.

The last war was the worst by far. We had such high hopes for the human that we found, the one *obsessed* with my people and the Underworld we are forced to occupy. We should have known that he was blatantly lying to us about being the Chosen One; we should have known better.

He'd constructed his own amulet, convincing us that it was real, that it would finally set us free. How naïve we were. All our combined years, and we'd let a fake fool us, so desperate for our freedom that we happily believed it was real, purely because we wanted out of our cage.

When the day finally came, when the portal opened, that was when we learned that it was all a lie. The amulet, the Chosen One, all of it was a lie. He'd been studying us for years, learning how we came to be, where we were, and he waited for his chance to prove that he was our king. And when he realized that he wasn't special, that he wasn't *anyone* at all, he had no choice but to lie. So desperate to be something, anything, in a world where he could be a little more than just a maggot.

That lie cost the lives of so many of my own kind, including family members who'd sacrificed themselves for the chance to save the rest. Lives lost for nothing. He didn't survive. Of course, he didn't. Before we were thrown back into the Underworld, we made sure to break his neck to teach him a lesson. It was less than he deserved, but it was all we could do.

This time. This time will be different. This time, I will find the Chosen One who can break this curse and save us all. But first, I need to break through this barrier.

"Stand back!" I warn my family.

I have to make sure the coast is clear first. The last thing we need is to breach the surface, only to be ambushed by armed humans waiting to kill us. I can't risk losing anyone else. Not after the loss of my father, not after he sacrificed himself the last time.

It's a tragedy I will always remember. I resent myself for not stepping up, taking his place. I failed him that day, but never again. I will keep the others safe in his memory and make sure no one else dies on my watch. Not if I can help it.

I reach a hand above my head, placing my palm against the concrete as I wait patiently. Or as patiently as I can when all I want to do is free myself of this living hell. I can feel the vibrations through my body, and as soon as I see that first crack of light, I move. I reach for it, fingers curling over the edge of the crack as I pull myself through, leaping out onto the surface and spinning around, motioning for my family to follow me.

The moment my feet touch the black asphalt, I'm struck by the feeling that this was how the ground *used* to feel like in the Underworld, solid and safe. I take a moment to look around. Everything is so different from the last time I was up here, and nothing is as I remember it.

The homes are more developed, stronger than they had been before, and a lot more of them. Made from red brick, an interesting choice. Metal contraptions with wheels cruise along well-paved roads, and large pyramid-shaped poles stick out of the ground, connected with wires from one to the next. The people walking around all carry small devices in their hands, staring at them intently as pictures move upon the faces of the thing they cradle, as if it's their own child.

I breathe a sigh of relief as I finally see something I do recognize. The familiar yellow and purple tones that have plagued my mind for centuries are still prevalent on the streets, despite how strange everything else looks and feels. It's almost comforting, almost, except I know what it means.

Something, other than the homes and how the people are acting, is different this time. Strangely quiet, like an animal waiting to pounce on its prey, leaving the weaker animal terrified of what is inevitable.

It strikes me as being too quiet, and I quickly look back to the doorway, realizing that none of my family members had joined me on the asphalt. The door is sealed shut.

"No, no, no!" I cry, clawing at the place the door had been mere moments ago, hoping to pry it open again and free my friends and family. But it's no use... they're still trapped down there, and I'm alone, left to face the humans alone. What have I done?

"Daddy, look! That man is all black!" I hear a child's voice call out, and I know he's talking about me.

"Kevin, stop that! Don't be rude." The father hisses.

I know what he's thinking, and I don't blame him, but it's not what the kid means.

I dart for the bushes that line the street, hiding out of sight and waiting until the father and son move away, grateful for the man's embarrassment as it means he doesn't want to linger longer than he has to. I look down at the dark skin on my hands, repulsed. I look as though my skin has been covered in oil. Thick, slick, and sickly.

This isn't what we planned. Centuries of organization, and everything has gone wrong; none of this was meant to happen. My family is supposed to be here with me, by my side, finding the Chosen One and destroying the humans. I can't do this alone. I don't have the strength to fight them all by myself.

CHAPTER 2

I hear a whistle, and I whip around, my gaze fixing on a man walking in my direction, alone. I smile. The perfect prey for my disguise, some good luck at last. I check that we're alone; no need to alert anyone as to what I'm about to do... or to the fact that I'm even here. Not yet, anyway.

Confident that we're alone, I lunge at him from behind the bushes, tackling the man to the ground. He screams and cries at my appearance as he struggles to free himself from my grasp, but I'm far stronger than he is, and his struggles are futile. I can see the way he's looking at me, but I can't say he looks much better, with his balding head and the beach ball barely contained by his hideous garments.

"Who are you? Wh-What are you?" He whimpers, eyes wide as he stares at me. "Please, don't hurt me. Someone, anyone, help!" His whining voice scrapes against my skull. For a man who looks like he could be a wrestler, a sumo wrestler anyway, he sure doesn't scream like one.

I try to conceal the disgust and pain that the shrieking tone of his voice causes me. I'm not willing to show any weakness to my prey, but that voice!

Even my little sister sounds less squeaky when she tries to summon an army of the dead, only to have that army turn on her seconds later. I've told her hundreds of times to not conjure an entire army when she can't even manage one hellhound. But she never listens. She has the strongest power out of all of us, but she can't control it.

Melanesia isn't like the rest of us. When the ground swallowed us five millennia ago, we didn't find ourselves alone. We stood in the presence of *real* demons, fire-breathing demons with claws sharp enough to rip open a grown human being and fling him into another universe entirely.

We were terrified and confused at first, faced with these creatures we'd only heard stories about for years, watching as they killed off so many of us. Those of us they spared, they accepted, molding us into their own. We learned to live with them for five thousand years, plotting our next move to take down the humans, but our goals were very different from theirs.

We wanted to redeem ourselves, to reclaim what was rightfully ours, and achieve our salvation. For them, sparing us and helping us was in exchange for our help when they asked for it, though they never did tell us what they wanted, and we didn't really care since all we wanted was to get our lives back.

That was how my sister was born. After my father died during our last attempt to overthrow the humans, my mother chose to remarry. To *him*. I'm not even really sure if demons *have* genders, or the known body parts that usually go with genders, but if any of them do, it's *him*. They're creatures of destruction, with magical abilities to reproduce in ways I've never really understood.

Asmodeus, my step-father, isn't exactly a saint. Other than Lucifer himself, Asmodeus is the most ruthless demon in the Underworld. He has no shame in eradicating anyone who crosses his path, or even looks at him weird. I remember once when one of my own dared to joke around and call him "Lord Ass" rather than "Lord Asmodeus," and I swear, I've never seen anyone liquify so fast before that moment. One snap of his fingers and gone, nothing left but a puddle of red goop that had once been someone I'd known. I learned to fear him, in my own way, and respect him in another.

It wasn't long before Melanesia was born. Half-human, half-demon. Powerful enough to levitate a small town after just one year of training, which is more dangerous than some of the fully-trained half-demons I'd been around. In a way, it's fortunate for this world that my sister still has a lot to learn. But then again, it isn't because we would have been able to beat the humans with ease if she could control her own powers. But we have a long way to go before Melanesia is going to be able to blink an eyelid and wipe humans out in the way her father wants her to.

My fist slams into the man's face, knocking him out cold with one hit. Maybe a little too cold... since he stops breathing immediately. I shrug; I don't care that he's dead.

"One less human to kill later," I mutter, throwing his limp body into the bushes behind me once I remove the items that I need.

Putting on his yellow coat and picking up his

purple umbrella, I roll my shoulders until the coat settles on me more comfortably. Hopefully, it will be enough to keep me unnoticed for a little while, until I can figure out how to open the door and let the rest of my kind out and onto the surface.

My family, my entire family, is still trapped in that abyss, and I'd much rather be there with them than here alone in my enemy's territory. It only takes one wrong look from someone, and I'll be as good as dead.

I'm strong. I like to pride myself on that, but without any real powers other than looking like a freak, there's no way I can defend myself on my own, let alone take out the humans. I don't think even Lucifer has the power to take on this town alone, not with the curse. It's why he needs us. I can speak telepathically through dreams, but then again, everyone in the Underworld can. It's how we learned to communicate without Lucifer finding out.

He's a tyrant and a dictator, and most of the conversations involve wishes to overthrow him and take over his kingdom. But sometimes, it's better to suck it up and do his bidding, rather than risk combustion. The phrase "better the devil you know" is pretty accurate. As awful as Lucifer is, we know who, and what, he is, but if someone like my step-father were to take over? Well... who knows what will happen to us?

They're just dreams, wishes that have to remain

wishes. After witnessing Eisheth, one of Lucifer's own, betray him like Judas betrayed Jesus, none of us dare go against Lucifer ever again.

I'll never forget that night when Lucifer discovered Eisheth's betrayal, the image of Eisheth's body incinerating under the raging inferno of Lucifer's flames, his eyeballs melting down his face. One minute he was there, and the next, a pile of ashes. It lasted minutes, in reality, but it felt as though hours had passed, and we were all scared.

But what good is dream telepathy, anyway? Hop into the dreams of my family, apologize for being a dick and leaving them all behind? I'm sure they'll all love that. I'm sure that would make up for the fact that I'm here, and they're not. As much as I hate my step-father, I wish I have the power that Asmodeus does. One evil stare, and the person he's looking at vanishes into nothingness, as though they were never there to begin with.

The rain is coming down hard and fast now, and I wonder how the humans deal with the constant wetness of their world, the cold that bites right into your very soul. Where I'm from, I know only heat. Hot and dry. That's it. I've been down there for so long that I barely remember what fresh air feels like. It's not the cleanest smell, but it's refreshing compared to the stench of death and decay that's suffocated me for longer than I dare admit.

I look down at my hands, like pools of the night sky giving form. All I can think about is that if I ever get my original skin back, I'm never complaining about being pale ever again.

I pull up the collar of the yellow coat and lower my head, pulling the umbrella down low so I can keep my face as hidden from others' view as much as possible. Given the strength of the rain, I'll be surprised if anyone can see my face well enough to notice the color of my skin, but I don't want to risk it, either.

"Howdy!" Suddenly, a man calls out to me in a jovial tone.

I automatically turn my head in his direction, twitching the collar again to ensure that the lower half of my face is covered by the yellow coat. The man is wearing a coat just like mine, and he carries the same purple umbrella. He waves at me with a smile, his round belly jiggling as he hurries along the path.

"It's really coming down out here! Best be heading home; don't want to get blown away now, do you?" He laughs to himself, and all I can do is roll my eyes.

"Yeah, sure." I force a chuckle from my throat, glancing back at the pavement rather than looking at him.

"My wife warned me about coming out on a day like this, but I couldn't help but run to the store for a six pack. You get it, us men and our needs." He chuckles, continuing to talk despite my clear disinterest.

If these humans didn't have weapons, their constant chatter and grating voices would be the death of me.

"You seem like you can use some cheering up, my friend. Care for a beer? I can survive on five for one night!" The man laughs again, his cackle beginning to make my brain bleed.

I finally look up at him and see that he's holding out a bottle with a strange yellow liquid inside. I catch his smile, so wholesome, so innocent, that for a moment, I almost forget that these humans are killers. I shake my head at him, rejecting his offer, but the smile remains on his face.

I don't want to be here. Not without my family.

I'm not here to make friends; I'm here for revenge.

"Suit yourself!" he replies in a sing-song voice. "But if you change your mind about that beer or get hungry, there's a great pub just a street down. I go there all the time." My eyes follow where the man points down the road toward the direction he'd just come from, and I look over my shoulder out of courtesy, trying not to draw attention to myself.

"Thanks," I mutter, watching the jolly plump man skip away.

My stomach begins to growl, and I silently curse

him for mentioning food. In the Underworld, the demons eat — they eat my kind, humans turned into monsters, who look more threatening than we really are. The reality is, we can't really defend ourselves, not really. It's why they pick us off, feeding their greedy, hungry bellies out of spite more than necessity, keeping us afraid so we remember our place.

The rest of us are left with the colorless gruel they serve the animals down there, twisted creatures that would just as readily eat us as the demons would. Thick gray gruel that looks and tastes like concrete — hard enough to kill someone if thrown at them. I don't even dare imagine what it's made from; I've never been brave enough to ask. I found the bone of a finger in it once, but I don't like to think about it for too long, or else it makes me feel sick.

Maybe eating something isn't a bad idea after all. I'm weak and lightheaded, and I'm alone in this world without the strength and support of my friends and family. I need to regain what little strength I have remaining. If they do attack, I don't have enough in me to fight back, and I have to stay alive. I have to stay safe for the sake of my family.

I have to make this right, and to do that, I have to find the Chosen One.

I turn around and stroll back down the way the man had pointed, keeping my head down to shield myself from the rain and keep my face hidden from all the other humans in yellow coats who glance in my direction. I don't know whether it's just paranoia, or whether they *are* all staring at me.

What the hell is so fascinating, anyway? I look just like everybody else in this godforsaken town — yellow and purple, my most hated colors in the whole universe. They're lucky I'm not my step-father. One look from him, and they'll all be gone. For good.

My stomach growls angrily at me the further down the road I get, so much so that I'm sure the people around me can hear it. The last thing I need is my stomach drawing attention to my presence. It's difficult enough to hide in plain sight as it is.

I clutch at my stomach as I continue down the road, searching for this infamous pub the man had been yammering about. I don't know what a beer is, but I'll happily take a bowl of barley and a glass of warm cow's milk. It's simple, and most would refer to it as "peasant" food, but to me, it would be the best meal in the whole world right now. *Anything* has to be better than the gray gruel I've been eating for the last thousand years.

I have no idea what this pub looks like. It's not a word I understand, but after a moment or two longer, a fragrant aroma wafts my way across the damp wind, and my stomach immediately answers with another, much louder, rumble. I stop, bending over slightly as I attempt to ignore the cramping in my belly, looking up at the sign above the door.

"Ge... Gera?" I try to make it out. "Whatever." What does it even matter? I don't even care; I just need food.

I don't want to hesitate. I don't want to show any sign of weakness, but at the same time, I'm afraid I'll be spotted and ambushed. As my stomach screams at me to fill it, I know I can't put it off anymore. I need to fill it, or I'll collapse from hunger, and then what will happen when they find me unconscious on the floor? Easy pickings for the enemy.

Driven inside by my need to stuff my face, the smell hits me hard. The delicious aroma mixes with something reminiscent of century-old wheat that's been left out to dry... and then rot in the sun. It reminds me of before, of home. It might not be the most pleasant smell, or the most pleasant memory, but it's more familiar than anything else in this world so far, and I cling to that.

"What can I get for you?" The man who speaks to me is scruffy, with wide blue eyes and a nose large enough that it feels like if he turned around too quickly, he would knock someone out with it. He nods his head at me as he wipes his pudgy, hairy hands on the dirty fabric around his waist, pulling a cloth from the pocket of the garment as he begins wiping down the surface in front of me. He then picks up the silver domes on the side and brushes away the crumbs from underneath them.

"Uh..." I hesitate, unsure of what to say, let alone what to ask for. I'm reminded of how different things are now since the last time my kind managed to reach the surface. I know nothing of this world. Keeping myself hidden is going to be difficult at the best of times, but it feels almost impossible right now.

"What? You gotta speak up, buddy. It's way too loud in here to be murmuring, and I'm hard of hearing." The man grunts at me, tapping at his ear.

"Ca-Can I get some food?" I ask stiffly, still keeping my voice low as though I expect the whole place to turn and stare at me if they hear me speak too loudly.

"Yeah, well, we got plenty of that here. What do you want? Burger? Cheesesteak? Fries? What?" he asks.

Burger? Cheesesteak? Fries? I don't recognize any of these words, but they don't sound like food to me. Before our incarceration, back when I was still a full human, I'd gotten used to the simple meals of barley, wheat, and what little I could manage to hunt with my own bare hands. I have no idea what a burger is. I have no idea if it's even alive or a plant. It's all completely new to me.

"Can I get a bowl of barley, please? And a glass of warm milk?" I ask, keeping my head low as I sit at the counter. My shoulders are slouched, and the hood of the yellow coat is pulled up over my head.

"Dude, what the hell are you talkin' about? This is a pub, not a farm. We ain't got none of that shit here. You want a burger or not?" the man asks angrily.

"Is... it is alive?"

The man laughs, patting his huge belly with a hand. "Ha! I hope not. Otherwise, I might have a lawsuit on my hands!" Suddenly, his smile turns into a scowl, and his eyebrows furrow as he stares at me. "Don't tell me you're one of those fucking vegans. All these Angelenos, always coming into my bar on their way to some dumbass festival or other lame event, asking for fucking tofu cheesesteaks and po-po bowls, or whatever is trending down there. Sick to death of it! Nothing wrong with a good bit of meat!"

I shake my head quickly, not wanting to draw any more attention to myself. I don't understand a word the man is saying, but as his cheeks turn red, I recognize human anger and realize it's best just to agree with him rather than make him angrier. If I ask any more questions, I'm only going to attract the attention of everyone else inside this stinky place, and I have to stay hidden for as long as I can.

"Good. Burger, then?" The man smiles again, his

anger forgotten, and I'm just grateful that whatever response I'd given him is the right one.

I nod, hoping that this "burger" is going to be enough to fill my aching stomach. I need to figure this new world out quickly so that I can fit in and hide until I can bring my family to me.

"One heart attack burger comin' right up! I swear, you haven't had a real burger until you've had a Geraldy's famous heart attack burger." The man leans in closer. "The secret is ten strips of the fattiest bacon you can find." He chuckles. "Little advice, buddy. Lay off the sunbeds. I don't know what kinda crazy voodoo pigment you got goin' on there, but I ain't ever seen that color on a man before." He laughs heartily.

I scowl slightly, shrinking under his gaze and pulling the coat tighter around me. Congratulations, Draven, as if this stupid yellow coat is ever going to be enough to hide me from the humans' sight. Nothing is *ever* going to be enough to conceal the monster that I am. Though, he hasn't immediately reached for a carving knife, so I should be glad of that small stroke of luck, I suppose.

My stomach continues to growl as he leaves me, and I take the opportunity to look around the room. It's noisy, despite there only being four to five humans in here, along with myself and the scruffy man. They don't look like the humans I remember, the ones who attacked and killed my father on sight. *They* had murder in their eyes, stern and evil; *they* were ready to kill us.

But these humans? These ones are insane; they're loopier than Asmodeus when he's had one chalice of blood too many. These humans, laughing and drinking something I don't recognize in excess, they're disconnected from reality in a way I don't understand. I wonder if these humans would even be able to destroy us demons; they're not at all like I remember them.

"Here you go, buddy. Your burger." The scruffy man returns and puts a fragrant round monstrosity down in front of me, pulling my attention away from these clowns I'm meant to be afraid of.

I turn my attention to the soft, spherical object, its delicious smell enticing me toward it, filling my brain with my hunger as I stare at this unusual thing in front of me. I reach out a finger and poke the top of it, smiling as it squishes down under the pressure of my finger.

"Heh. Squishy," I mutter. "Of course, it is. I'd break my teeth otherwise." I roll my eyes at myself, wondering how I even manage to function some days.

The scruffy man snorts in amusement, raising an eyebrow at me as he watches me interact with my burger. "What's the matter? Never seen a burger before?" he asks me.

I shake my head, suddenly feeling very conscious of that fact. Clearly, it's an odd thing not to have had, which only makes me stick out like a sore thumb.

"You know, you're a very, very peculiar man. Skin dark as ash, walkin' around in a daze, asking for barley and milk. You're definitely not from around here, but I like it, and I've decided that I like you." He chuckles, pointing to the burger still squished underneath my finger. "Try it. You'll love it; trust me."

I reach down to take the burger in my hands, watching as its juices drip down onto the plate below, the smell making my mouth water. Licking my lips, I take a large bite out of the soft thing, flavor flooding my tongue as my saliva fills my mouth at the delectable taste. I swallow and let out a soft moan of pleasure as I smile at the man.

"Like it?" he asks, though I can tell by his face that he already knows the answer.

"This is the best thing I have ever tasted in my life," I reply with a nod.

"Knew you'd like it; everyone always does. Unless they're one of those stupid vegans." He snorts. "Don't got no business being in my life if you don't like burgers." He adds with a nod. "Tell ya what, seein' as this is the first time you've had one, it's on the house."

"On the house?" I ask, not understanding why the burger would be on the house.

He laughs and claps a hand on his belly. "You really are something, you know that? On the house! Free of charge! You just enjoy that, and don't worry about havin' to pay me." He smiles.

My face feels hot as my cheeks flush red. I feel like such an idiot, though I'm grateful the man finds my clear naivety amusing rather than irritating. I know absolutely nothing of what the world is now, and it's evident to this man, as well as to me.

These people are idiots, all of them. I can't believe my luck; I'd expected to spend my time running and hiding, fighting for my life, but these people are oblivious to what I really am. They don't see me as a threat at all, and that's going to work out in my favor.

I can't let my true colors show, not just yet, but at least it's doubtful that these fools will even realize who or what I am, too dumb to realize what they're looking at or why I don't understand their simple phrases. I can't forget my mission, either. There's too much at stake, and my family needs me.

I stay at the pub for an hour or so, letting the scruffy man chat me up while he's still happy to do so, and while he's content to feed me free food, having discovered that I know very little of their cuisine. It took a little stretching of the truth for him to understand that "where I came from," we ate very plain foods, and that such exotic meals are foreign to me.

He seems nice enough, but I'm also not naïve enough to believe that he won't turn on me the moment he realizes what I am. For the brief moment that he's useful, he's fueling me and helping me regain my strength. He's also teaching me a little more about this world, but beyond that, he'll still end up dying by my hands when the time comes.

After leaving the pub, I spend several hours wandering around the streets, looking for signs of something I'm not even sure exists anymore. I'm drained and ready to give up, the strain of being alone weighing heavily upon me as I walk these unfamiliar streets alone. My family has always been my backbone, my support system, and without them, I feel utterly lost.

Knowing that they're trapped down there, that they couldn't get out when I did, tears at my heart, and I feel nauseous. The food I had just eaten churns in my stomach at the thought of my family clawing at the ground above their heads, trying to join me here on the surface.

Everywhere I go, I'm surrounded by yellow coats and purple umbrellas, each person passing me by with either a smile or a look of disgust, but none of the hatred I expected to find when I pulled myself free from the Underworld. I'm not sure which look I prefer from these humans, the disgust or the absurd smile.

I look up at the sky as I stand on a gross knoll beneath the trees, the rain splattering across my face. It's growing dark now, the day finally turning to night, a chance for me to blend in, thanks to my dark skin. The moon and stars shine above me, glowing brightly in a way I'd almost forgotten, so used to the cavernous hell of molten lava that had been home for the last few millennia.

The cold wind beats the rain down hard on me, and I shiver as it grips my skin with its icy fingers. I haven't felt cold in so long that I'd forgotten what it feels like. It feels so peaceful out here, beautiful in its own way, making me feel as though my life is a little less chaotic...

CHAPTER 3

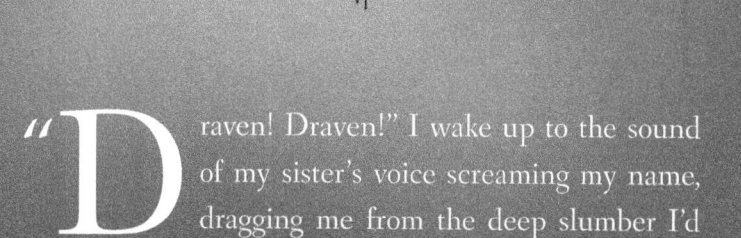

"Draven! Draven!" I wake up to the sound of my sister's voice screaming my name, dragging me from the deep slumber I'd finally managed to get into.

"Huh?" I whisper as I stir, blinking and looking around myself, still on the grassy knoll beneath the trees where I had stopped to look at the night sky above me. It's still dark, and I look around frantically, finding nothing but the tree branches blowing in the wind, and the large drops of rain still falling from the sky.

"Melanesia? Is that you? Where are you?" I call out to her, my heart pounding in my chest as I try to see where she's hiding, searching for a shadowy figure that could be my sister.

"Up here, sweetie," another voice calls me, calmer and more mature, "look up."

My eyes dart to the sky above me, filled with stars and dark clouds, my mother and sister smiling down at me and waving.

"Mom? Melanesia?"

"Yes, sweetie, it's us. We're here. We came to check on you, to make sure you're safe." My mother replies in her soft, loving tone, making my heart ache as all I want to do is hold her.

"What happened?" I ask, forcing myself not to cry or show her any fear — I don't want her to worry any more than she probably already has been. "Why didn't the rest of you follow me?"

"We tried, sweetheart, we tried. But everyone was pushing us. They created a block in the doorway, and by the time any of us could get free enough to pull ourselves through, the doorway had closed on us. It didn't stay open as long as it usually does," my mother replies, a sadness in her tone.

"Yeah, why'd you run off so fast, Draven? Mother

was afraid the humans would just murder you at first sight. I'm surprised you're still alive," Melanesia chimes in cheerfully. She's still young and somewhat naïve, and still finds death and destruction fascinating — she truly is her father's daughter in that respect. There's less of my mother in her than there is Asmodeus, and it's terrifying.

"Melanesia, stop that!" my mother snaps at her, chiding her daughter.

"Sorry," my sister whispers.

I still find it miraculous that my sister will listen to anyone other than her father, given the power that she holds, but she seems to love and respect our mother enough to behave herself when told. Though, I don't know how long that will last, not once my sister figures out how to control her powers, and she realizes that she doesn't really need to listen to mother at all.

My eyes meet my mother's, and I can see the relief on her face. Like Melanesia said, mother had been worried. I feel a little better knowing that she clearly doesn't hate me for getting out while they're all still stuck in the Underworld. I'm just glad she can reach out to me this way.

"I'm glad you're okay, but there's no turning back now. You know that, don't you? The surface won't open for us again until you find the Chosen One, sweetheart. Whoever that may be. You have to find them, Draven, and reopen the portal for us all to follow you, Otherwise, I'm afraid you're stuck up there without us, separated for another thousand years until the portal opens again on its own."

"What about Lucifer? I'm sure *he* has the power to crack the surface." It's a question we've all wanted to ask but never quite dared to. However, now that I'm alone, he can't do me any harm for speaking out against him *unless* he comes up here to give me a lesson. And if he does, the others can follow him. Win-win.

My mother shakes her head, looking sad again. "No, not even Lucifer has the power to manipulate the portal that separates the Earth and the Underworld. Otherwise, he would have marched his armies against the humans long ago. It's up to you, Draven. I know it's a lot to ask of you, but we all believe in you. Jeziah says the Chosen One will be a green-eyed belle who wears a pentagram ring. Find her, sweetie. Find her, and save us all."

"Yeah, Draven. Don't fuck it up." Melanesia snaps at me, wincing as mother glares at her for swearing. "You're our only hope," she adds in a slightly less bossy tone.

"Geez, thanks. No pressure, then," I mutter, watching as the vision of my mother and sister wavers and vanishes from the sky, leaving me all alone once again. I should never have expected any compassion from my sister; it had never been her strength. It's not her fault, being what she is. Her empathy is pretty stunted. It never really existed for the demons, and unfortunately, the human half from my mother is tainted by our current situation... not that I think it would have made much difference where Melanesia is concerned.

With my family gone again, I sigh, shivering in the wind and the rain as the cold seeps back in without the distraction that my family's presence offered for a moment. I wrap my arms around myself as I try to stop the shivering, but it's no use; I'm soaked. I never thought I'd miss the heat from the Underworld, and all those things I loathed when I was stuck in that place, the familiarity, the understanding.

Now I'm cold and alone, acutely aware that if I die here from freezing to death, that my family will never get out this time and will face another thousand years trapped beneath the surface, clawing at the black ground above their heads.

I pull myself to my feet and slip down the grassy hill, hugging the purple umbrella close over my head, though at this point, it feels superfluous as I'm already wet. I run, in no particular direction, until I find myself staring at the face of a mountain, its surface pockmarked with more crevices and scars than I have on my entire body. I need to find shelter, and the nooks and caves on the surface are perfect for what I need. I pick the nearest one and rush inside.

The ground below my feet is soft, the soil squishy, reminding me again of how the ground in the Underworld had felt before I escaped. It's empty, except for a couple of squeaking rats, but I don't mind sharing my space with them. At least, I'm not alone. It's warm and dry, and for now, it's sheltered and will suffice until the morning.

"Draven! Draven, please, don't leave us! Don't leave us!" My mother is crying behind me, but I'm too far ahead to turn back now. If I do, it's all for nothing.

"They're killing us! Brother, help us!" Melanesia's cries are like a dagger to my heart, her fear setting my teeth on edge.

Her desperation causes me to turn around, and I reach my hand out to her, but my hand is rebuffed by a transparent barrier, separating me from my family all over again. I watch in despair as the humans tear into my family, stabbing them with swords, blood and gore dripping from the ends of their blades as they slice my mother's head clean from her shoulders. I'm so close, yet too far away, unable to help, frozen in horror as I watch my family die, crying hard as I collapse to my knees, rocking back and forth as I bite back the rising nausea.

Melanesia emerges from the massacre, her eyes black, bloodied voids where her eyeballs should have been, blood dripping down her cheeks like red tears of despair. "You left us, brother. You left us here to die; it's all your fault!"

"No!" I scream, waking up from my nightmare in a sweat, my heart pounding painfully in my chest as I gasp for breath. I'm alive, and so are they. I know it deep down, but that horrible nightmare lingers in my mind, the image of my family covered in blood harassing me the moment I close my eyes.

I stumble to my feet, leaning heavily against the cold cave wall to support my weight as my legs tremble beneath me, threatening to send me crashing to the floor again. I grab the yellow coat from the rock where I'd left it the previous night to dry, clutching at the umbrella with a trembling hand, willing my fingers not to lose their grip.

I can focus on the small things. I can do this to ground myself, to diminish the images of a fate that I fear more than anything else.

Staggering from the cave, I gasp, gulping in huge breaths of fresh air as the rain slaps against my exposed face. It's still pouring down. I'm not surprised, but I'm not happy about it, either. I'd considered going down to the canal I spotted on my way to the mountain and splashing water on my face, but it's unnecessary with the endless rain. Dark clouds loom overhead, the raindrops like heavy, wet bullets as they pound against the ground and anything in their way, me included.

There's no sun, and I have no clue what time it is, but I also don't care. All I can think about is finding the Chosen One and saving my family. That's all that matters now — they're counting on me, but every second without knowing who the Chosen One is, feels like a knife to the heart, and the despair I feel at being alone dares to creep back in again.

I make my way to the canal anyway, my mind so full of my family that my father creeps into my thoughts, and I remember the days spent skipping rocks across the water with him, happy with the simple joy of counting how many skips each we managed to get, counting the ripples that were made when we threw the bigger rocks into the depths of the water.

Nature has always fascinated me, but in all this rain, I'm losing count of the ripples as each raindrop casts their own rings across the turbulent surface of the canal.

As I reach the water's edge, I realize that I'm not as alone as I first thought I was. A girl, wearing a white top and blue bottoms, leans back into the dense puddle behind her without a care in the world, as though she doesn't even realize it's raining at all. She's soaked, her top clinging to her skin, her brown hair dangling behind her in wet strands that nearly touch the ground.

The sight of her makes my cheeks flush, but I doubt anyone could see the color against my dark skin. And my eyes. My eyes are drawn to the hard nubs of her nipples, pressing against her top in the cold, damp weather. It's been so long since I've seen anyone so beautiful, and the way she doesn't care attracts me immediately and without reason.

Love is meaningless to my people. My mother married Asmodeus out of the pure need to survive, not out of affection — but as I gaze upon this woman, I have a vague recollection of what romance was from when I was still human, what it feels to be attracted to someone for reasons other than to survive.

I'm drawn to her, fascinated as she picks up a rock and tosses it into the water in front of her, watching the ripples, just as I had been. I think I love her already, this beautiful creature before me. I want to see her face, but I'm afraid of her seeing me for what I really am — she's human; she'll kill me on the spot. Though so far, none of the others have, but the fear remains, especially after my nightmares.

I hear her move, and I dive behind a bush, hiding in

the foliage as she gets up and starts to walk away. As she moves closer to me, she reaches into her backpack, but that's not what catches my eye. It's the flash of something on her finger... and then I see it.

The ring. The *pentagram* ring. She looks toward my direction, and I catch sight of her eyes for the first time — deep emeralds that glisten even in this darkness. She's the Chosen One! I've found her!

I knew there was something special about her! What other person would be out in this weather without a coat or an umbrella? Unlike the rest of this strange town, she's not sporting the yellow coat and purple umbrella that seem to be almost required by the residents, and like me, I feel like she doesn't belong here anymore than I do. It's meant to be; it's fate.

My heart races so loudly in my chest that I'm afraid she might hear it, but she doesn't, walking alone in the rain and vanishing around the corner. Oblivious to my existence. I don't question it, for now I'm grateful.

I have to be cautious, however. I have to take things slow and get her on my side. As much as I want to grab her and beg her to help my family, I know that this could drive her further away and lead to my death... and then what? Another thousand years of waiting for my family because I'd been too impatient to coax the Chosen One to our side?

Keeping my distance, I follow her, determined to keep my eye on her. I can't lose her. I need to make sure I know where she is so that I can start to bring her around to our side, to make her see that what's been done to us is unfair. She never even looks back, never suspects that someone's following her, but why would she? Out here, in this sea of yellow coats and purple umbrellas, *she* is the odd one out, not me. I've got my disguise, pathetic as it may be, but it's enough to protect me from any immediate scrutiny, and it lets me blend in enough that she doesn't even bother to look back at me.

Once she's home, I wait, listening to the voices inside the home, keeping as still and hidden as I can until I know where she is. Despite the cold, despite the rain, I pull off the yellow coat and flatten the umbrella, hiding them in one of the garden bushes, ready to retrieve them if, and when, I need to. For now, my dark skin is my camouflage. I may hate it, but it's useful for the time being.

A voice, feminine and melodic, drifts from one of the back windows, and I hurry around the side of the house, pulling myself up the lattice fence that's nailed onto the side with ease until I'm at her window ledge, protected from the rain by the roof, able to sit and listen as I blend into the shadows of the house under the darkened sky.

I can't hear who she's talking to, but I can hear her side of things, enough to know that she's talking to a boy and that her name is Bella Nova. I instantly hate him. Millennia of hatred for humans boiling over and spilling into a grudge against the boy at the other end of that conversation, despite him not being in the room with her. I know she's not mad; she's holding one of those silly objects I'd seen when I first arrived to her head and talking into it, though I don't really understand what it is. He's my rival, though he doesn't yet know it.

My heart aches in my chest as I see her smiling from her bed, and all I want to do is reach out and touch her, wondering what it would feel like to kiss her lips. Her eyes glitter like emeralds, and I'm jealous of the boy she's so happily enjoying a conversation with. He's not a man, not in my eyes. If he were, he would have been here in person to say whatever sweet nothings he's uttering to her through the strange device. Only a coward would say such things from afar.

I shiver, wishing I had some warmer clothing to wear, but the coat is too bright, and she would surely see me if I were to wear it while I watched her. I need to know more about her, need to be closer to her and understand who she is. I need to make her understand that she's our only hope of ever reclaiming what's rightfully ours.

I wait for her to fall asleep, knowing that my best chance to interact with her is through dream telepathy. It's the easiest way to speak without her immediately threatening my life, and this way, I can know her innermost thoughts as well. Her dreams are restless, and I realize what I'm watching is a memory, rather than a nightmare that her mind has made up — the details are too clear, too precise to be a dream.

I see the man hurting her, and I want to step forward and tear him apart. I need her, in more ways than one, and I cannot afford for him to hurt her — but I can't do anything. This has already happened, but at least I know about it.

Seconds before she wakes up, I feel a thought drift across her mind, that she wishes the memories would go away, even for a moment, and I smile to myself. That's my window; that's how I reach her. I steal those dreams from her and replace them with my own.

Bella Nova, you will be mine.

I CHOOSE to sleep during the day, leaving Bella to go about her day while I rest and get my head back on straight. I settle back into my cave and concentrate on my breathing, closing my eyes and drifting off, reaching out to my family as I do so.

The Underworld is a cavernous place of black rock, sharp and porous like lava cooling over time, though there are still rivers of lava glowing throughout the entire place, the black ground of the layer above us like a perpetual night sky. I've spent millennia dreaming about getting out of this place, and now that I'm standing here, a dream-self, all I want is to be back with my family in the stifling heat.

"Draven!" My mother's voice calls to me as she sees me standing close by, and she hurries to me with Melanesia beside her. "What's wrong?"

"I've found her. I've found the Chosen One."

"Then why are you *here*?" Melanesia rolls her eyes at me, arms crossed over her chest as she gives me her best glare, much like Asmodeus would... though if it were him, I'd be dead.

"To *tell* you that I've found her." I roll my eyes at her in return. "I'm going to work on her tonight. I'll get her on our side. I just wanted to let you know."

"Be quick, sweetie. I don't like you being up there all on your own."

I smile and nod, but I say nothing else. I know I'm alone. I don't need reminding, and I certainly don't want to think about it. I also don't want to think about how long it might take me to get Bella on our side either, but I can only do what I can do.

I leave the dream behind and rest, waking up and making my way back down the mountain and into town under the cover of night. It's time. I climb up the lattice fence to Bella's window, smiling at her sleeping face as I reach out to her dreams like I did the night before, inserting myself into them this time.

"Bella, Bella Nova," I call to her softly in her dream.

"What? Who is it? Who's here?" she replies.

I can hear the fear in her voice, but I need her. I need her to listen.

The world around us reflects the only world I've known for the last five millennia, the world of the Underworld, all black and red and full of nightmares that she can't possibly imagine.

"Hello?" she calls out to me again in an uncertain tone, wary, afraid, but I don't have time to be gentle or kind — I need her now.

She looks around, but she doesn't see me, and I fear that she's unable to see me, that my connection isn't strong enough. She starts to walk away from me, and my heart leaps into my chest as I reach out to her, our connection growing weaker.

"Bella, Bella!" My voice is drowned out by another, and she's pulled away from me.

Dragged from the dream, I open my eyes and quietly curse as her mother shakes her awake. I don't have time to waste. I'm going to have to be more aggressive in my approach if I want to get her to listen to me. My family is counting on me. I cannot waste any more time.

CHAPTER 4

Watching him kiss her, I imagine what it would feel like to rip his head straight off from his shoulders, but I know better. There's no point in killing him, not yet anyway, not in front of Bella. I need her on my side, and killing her *precious* boyfriend would only turn her against me entirely. He can have today, can spend it with her and touch her, but he won't get anymore. After tonight, I intend to make her mine, and I won't stop until she is.

I return back to my cave for the day after stopping at the pub for a quick meal with my strange new friend, the man who owns the place. He seems to have taken a liking to me, or he pities me. Whichever it is, I don't care. He feeds me for nothing, and I'm not going to scoff at that.

He looks at me, but I don't think he *sees* me. I don't think any of them do. It's as if they're oblivious to what I really am. Either that, or their inability to believe in our kind has left them blind to what's staring them straight in the face.

Whatever the reason, I don't care. It means I can move a little more freely and without worry, as these ignorant humans genuinely seem unaware of what now walks amongst them. If my family were here, we could have defeated these weak fools with ease, but on my own... the minute I dare to try could be my undoing. I'm alone here, and while I *could* take them on, they would begin to fight back. What use would I be to my family then?

I dream of my family while I sleep, nightmares that wake me violently and leave me drenched in sweat, the faces of my family imprinted in my memory and on my eyes, even as I stare at the blank cave wall, gasping for breath as the sweat beads down my back. It's always the same dream. My failure resulting in my family being stuck in the Underworld for another millennia, or them getting to the surface and being slaughtered while all I can do is watch helplessly. I refuse to let my dreams become reality. I can't let that happen to my family. They're already suffering because of me, and I can't let them down again.

Dragging myself from my current shelter, I make my way back to Bella's home, my heart calling me to her window, instinctively drawn to her very existence. I watch as she kisses the corsage that *he* clearly gave her, and I instantly want to tear it to shreds with my hands. He has her heart at the moment, but it won't last; I'll make sure of it. Soon, she will be mine, and he will be nothing but a distant memory. A bad smell she wishes to forget. How could she ever want him over me?

I want her to slip into bed, to go to sleep so that I can join her in her dream. It's as close to her as I can be right now, but anything is better than nothing until I can persuade her to help me and my family. I watch her bend over her desk, working on something I don't truly understand, let alone remotely care about.

"Please, Bella, I need you to sleep. I need you to see me," I whisper quietly, my breath fogging up her window as I watch her longingly.

All I want to do is gather her in my arms and kiss

her, taste her on my lips. The thought of her body pressed against mine arouses me, and I groan softly at the thought of her bare skin against mine. I shift comfortably, my cock pressing hard against my bottoms. I've not felt like this for over five thousand years, not felt the call of my sexual instincts, let alone met anyone who has brought them to the surface like she does. I know it's stupid and dangerous to let her distract me, but I can't think of anything else as I watch her breathe slowly, her shoulders shifting gently with the movement as she works.

I want to take her by her shoulders, spin her around, and kiss her in such a way that she fears I may devour her in my need to touch her. I wouldn't, but the growing need in my heart and bottoms would suggest otherwise.

Finally, she rises from her chair, giving me a welcoming distraction from the tingling sensation in my groin that aches to be satiated. I watch her with eager eyes as she collapses onto her bed, asleep the instant her head hits the soft pillow, and I know that it's my chance at last. *My* chance to be with her. I close my eyes and will my racing heart to slow its pace. The vigorous drumbeat is too distracting for what I need to do. I close my eyes and picture her face, her dreams, like I did before, until I wake up to find myself in the shadows of her mind.

"Bella, Bella Nova," I call to her, almost shocked by the deep, reverberating sound of my own voice as though I've forgotten what I sound like. I try not to be nervous about being close to her, but I can't help it. I love her. I *need* her.

I hear her cry out in pain and immediately want to rush to her, pull her into my arms and keep her close and safe. I know I can't approach her, not yet. I need her to seek *me* out. So, when she does, when she tells me to show myself and stop playing games, I do as she asks, sort of. Hands clenched into fists to stop myself from trembling, I turn a corner behind a large boulder. I *know* she will follow me because, of course, she will. She wants answers, and I want her to want me.

She does exactly as I expect her to, running around the boulder, thinking I'm waiting there. But of course, I'm not. I need her to keep chasing me. The more I'm a mystery, the more she will want me.

I can feel her frustration as she finds that I'm not there waiting for her as she'd expected, and I can't help but smile, my heart pounding in my chest again as I wait for her to realize that I'm actually behind her. Finally, she sees me, *me*, all of me as I truly am. It shouldn't hurt as much as it does when she yelps and steps away from me, her eyes wide and filled with fear at the sight of the monster I am because of a simple and arrogant mistake I made long ago.

Lost in her eyes, I lose my voice, forgetting how to speak as I stare into the deep, green pools staring back at me. Finally, she speaks, and it's like music to my ears because she's talking to *me*. I feel as though I might float away with happiness that she can finally see me, that I'm the one who has her attention... until she says *his* name. I'm not angry with her. I don't think I can be, but I feel as though her fingers are digging into my heart and ripping it into two.

I step toward her and reach out on impulse, my hand resting against her cheek, freezing there as I feel her warmth under my fingers, but as she says his name again, I shake my head, swallowing the hurt and my pride. It's time, time to make her mine.

"My name is Draven Asmodeus. I am a demon of the Underworld, and I need your help."

She whispers the word "Hell," and then she's gone from the dream, from my grasp, and even as I reach for her, I know I'll have to try again. Time is running out for my family, and I need to make Bella understand. I need her to work with me so that I can save them. But everything hinges on her. Everything.

I gasp as I return to the waking world, watching her leave her room and return again a moment later to go back to sleep. She's exhausted, and so am I. Pushing my intention, my need, on her is tiring, even for such short periods of time, and I know I'm getting desperate. I have to try harder.

Tomorrow night. Tomorrow night, I *have* to make her understand. I can still feel her on my hand, where my fingertips stroked her cheek, and I moan softly at the thought of touching the rest of her skin, of hearing *her* moan with pleasure because of *me*. I have to stay close to her. I need her as much as I need to breathe. I can't fail again. I need to make her see me.

I CAN BARELY SLEEP during the day, Bella haunting my every thought, replacing the nightmarish images of my family being slaughtered with the far sweeter image of her in my arms. She left me restless, wanting more, longing for the dream to become a reality. The erection pressing against my clothes is uncomfortable and aches for release, but I know I have to wait. Not that it stops me from dreaming of her again, naked and sweating beneath me as I slide into her and feel her writhe against my body.

When I return to her house, this time, I'm reminded of those dreams, of the way her skin felt against my hand the night before, and the feeling of her naked body pressed against mine, the electric tingle my imagination came up with that I'm convinced was real. I want her; I need her. The more I think about it, the more I love her.

Focus! I hiss to myself. I'm so caught up in what I want that I can't focus on what I need to do. *He's* there with her, courting her in the way that I should be, and it gives me something to cling to. Hatred is a powerful emotion, one that demons are more than a little familiar with. Asmodeus taught us all how to use our anger and hatred, concentrating on it in order to strengthen ourselves and our powers. That's what I need to remember. I need to hate the other boy for being the one she sees right now. I need to hate the humans for what they did to my family, and I need to make Bella see me.

I take a deep breath and close my eyes, staying close to Bella in her dream and watching as the boy smiles at her. The fire in my heart is kindled by that look, a raging inferno that, one day, I swear will burn him from the Earth the moment my family is free. Bella will be mine, and he will become nothing but a speck of dust in the wind.

With the ball of hatred now a painful fist around my heart, I know it's time, time to reach across the dream and break the barrier. I need Bella to hear me this time. I was so close last time, but I *have* to make her understand how important she is, more so than this idiotic human brat can ever understand.

"HELP ME!" I scream, the box that Bella's in shaking around her with the force of my voice and my intention, my desperation for her to hear *me* over him. I hear her call out his name in fear, but I don't care. I'm not going to fail this time. This time, she is *going* to hear me, and she is *going* to see me.

My heart pounds in my chest as I force myself into her dream. I claw my way into his place, melting him, turning him to ash — a foreshadowing of exactly what I'm going to do to him once Bella is on our side, once the Chosen One is mine. This dream? This perfect fantasy of hers? I tear it away and show her the helpless, burning nightmare my family suffers with every day of their lives because of *one* mistake.

We all get told that we get a second chance, a chance where we can redeem ourselves for whatever wrongs we did in our past. But *we* never got that chance. *I* never got that chance, so now I'm taking it.

I stand there on the burning asphalt I've called home for five thousand years, but not by choice. I hate bringing her here as much as I hate that this is where my family is trapped, but I need Bella to understand. I need her to *see* what is happening to my people. If she sees this, if she fears it and hates it as much as we do, then she is more likely to help us.

I know she's a kind person. I can see that from the moment I met her. She has a big heart, and she's been hurt before, but I know she's the Chosen One for a reason. The others, the fake ones and the useless ones, they were *never* the real chosen ones, not ever. Bella. It was always Bella, and the ones who came before her. Her ancestors.

I see that now. And all the suffering we've been through, all the nightmares and the hell I've lived through, will be worth it because of her.

"Welcome back, Bella," I whisper as I step around the rock where she last saw me. "I've been expecting you."

"Who are you? And what do you want from me?" Her voice is like music to my ears, even as she shouts at me, because at least her attention is directed at *me*.

"You're the Chosen One, the one our leader has prophesied would come and finally save us, finally set us free. You are the only one who can help us." My heart aches as she turns away from me. I don't blame her for being scared, and why would I? Even though I can't stand how I look and what I am now, I can't stop. I can't let her turn away from me again.

"I can't help you! I can't! I can't even help myself. Please, whoever you are, leave me alone! Leave me alone! Leave me alone!" Her voice tears at my heart, and all I want to do is reach out to her and hold her close.

I know this is terrifying, and I know I'm asking a lot from her, but she's our only hope, *my* only hope. I'm thrown back into reality again, left trembling and panting as I stare at her through her window, wishing that she would stop pushing me away. Every time, I get a little closer, but it's taking too long, and her rejections are like a knife to the heart, a knife twisting each time I'm thrown from her dreams.

I gasp for breath, a clawed hand pressed to my heaving chest as I force myself to breath, my heart thundering against my palm. I wonder if a heart can escape a person's body from beating too fast, because if it could, mine's about to. I watch her as she reaches for her phone, and I know she's calling him again. The beat of my heart slows as the icy tendrils of hatred creep into the back of my mind. I can't hear his voice, but I know he's there, regardless. I never realized I could hate someone more than I hate Asmodeus, or Lucifer, or even myself for my failings. But him? My resentment toward him is more than anything I can describe.

Scowling, I hook a claw under her window and open it before I even think about what I'm actually doing. I slip into her room and slink into the shadows, breathing heavily as I watch her on her bed. She's so close to me now, and I realize the significance of where I'm standing.

She's not getting away from me, not this time. I don't care that he has her heart. If she gives me the chance, I know I can show her how much more of a man I am than this pathetic *boy* of hers. As soon as she hangs up, I can't help but smile. I swear, she's going to hear me this time, and this time, she won't have a choice.

"Hello, Bella."

"Whoa!" she cries out, almost falling off her bed as she hears me speak.

I'm no longer a dream; I'm a reality. Her flashlight doesn't find me at first, and I know it's because her mind won't *let* me be real to her. That's why the other humans don't "see" me, not really, because they no longer believe in demons.

At least, the humans I've met so far don't, though I'm sure there are still plenty in this godforsaken town who believes in us, and it's them I have to avoid.

After a second, she stops and throws her hands over her mouth in fear. There. There it is; she can finally see me.

"Please, leave me alone," she whispers, hiding beneath her blanket as though, somehow, that's enough of a defense against something of my magnitude. She closes her eyes, and I move from my spot by the wall, closing the distance between us.

I reach out and grab her wrist, pulling her toward me. I can't wait any longer. I need her to stop hiding from me. She kicks me away, and for the moment, I let her, fading back into the half-reality of existence that I've been in with her for a little while. But that's okay. I'm getting closer now. She can't hide from me anymore, not really, not again.

I'm in her head.

CHAPTER 5

I'd touched her. Not just in a dream, where my imagination can run rampant, but something real. It's more than I ever believed was possible. All this time, all those millennia where I never felt anything for anyone. It wasn't something that was important to me, getting my family free from their nightmare was and still is, because it was my fault that they're trapped in this horror in the first place.

I stare at my hand, tracing my palm with my finger. I didn't mean to fall in love with her. I know that my family was meant to be here with me so that we could take back what's rightfully ours, but I can't help how I feel.

She's seen me now. She's felt my hand on her arm, and I've left a mark. I never meant to hurt her, but part of me is also happy about it as well. My handprint is on her arm, marking her forever, reminding her that I'm always with her. Things are real for her now, and I need to keep it real so that she cannot keep pushing me away.

I hate that I'm going to have to hurt her first, but I promise I'll make it up to her, that I'll make everything right again. She wants to deny what she's seen, and something deep inside me understands that. Why would anyone want something like me to be real? But I need to be real to her, so that I can save my family once and for all.

This time, I won't leave. This time, I'm going to stay close to her. I'm going to drive her mad, make her angry, and force her to face me, just as I used my anger toward that dumb boy of hers to become real. She can only deny me for a little while. The more I subject her to my presence, unwanted or otherwise, the more likely it is that she will confront me, and then we can finally *talk*. I need her to listen to me so that I can get her help.

My body aches from the force of my intention coming into her reality the way it did, and part of me desperately wants to slink back into my cave and sleep, but I can't bear to leave Bella now. At the back of my mind, I'm aware that I'm following her around like some uninvited shadow, especially into private places like when she's bathing.

Of course, I'm curious. How can I not be? I'm dying to see her naked, to touch her, and make her moan in pleasure. I've never been with a woman like her, and I can barely contain my need for her.

She looks in the mirror as she dries her face with a towel, and she *sees* me. I smile, as softly as I can. I don't want to admit how glad I am when she jumps and screams. I know I shouldn't be. It's not the ideal reaction to her seeing my face, but it means she cannot ignore me now. She can push me away all she likes, but I'm a part of her world now, and I'm not going anywhere.

Where Bella goes, I go. I can see her trying not to look for me in every reflection, keeping her head down as though staring at the floor rather than looking over her shoulder might make me go away. She has two shadows now, and there is no way I'm leaving her side unless I have to... or unless I really start to push too hard too fast.

She's meeting with *him* again; of course, she is. I

hardly expected her to stop seeing him *just* because she's seen me, but it doesn't hurt any less when he kisses her and touches her in all the ways I want to.

"You look like you've seen a monster."

I can't help but grin fiendishly at the words that slip from his tongue, and I'm glad when Bella bites back with her own words. Good. He's not little Mister Perfect, and she's going to realize how much better off she'd be with me. He has *no* idea how truthful his words are, but it doesn't matter; I'm going to make him eat them before long.

There's something satisfying at his faux pas, and I can't stop grinning as I slide into the back of the car, technically too big for it given my horns — but such things don't worry me too much.

Spotting my reflection in the car mirror frightens her, though I'm hardly surprised at this reaction. The car swerves, and I delight a little in the boy's loss of control, and the fact that he gets frustrated with Bella.

That's it. Push her away; show her that she can't count on you. I coax softly, willing him to show Bella how truly insensitive he can be. I was never concerned about the car. *Had* the idiot lost control, I would have saved Bella myself. Of course, I would.

I watch carefully as the boy sighs at Bella, clearly not believing her as he climbs back into the car and starts driving again. It's hard not to laugh at him, to know that soon enough, I'm going to take her from him. Leaning forward, I gently run my black nails through her hair, sighing softly as I enjoy the feeling, until she pulls away from me.

I'm a little surprised at my own confidence. I've never been this bold, relying on my father and mother for strength, but I want her. The more I think about being with her, the harder it is to resist pushing her to her limit so that she will reach out to me. She stares at me, and all I can do is grin.

Soon. Soon, she'll be mine.

I DRAG my feet behind me, forcing myself to move my legs one in front of the other as I slump toward my cave. Try as I might, I cannot ignore the exhaustion that's seeping into my bones. Everything aches. The strain from forcing myself into Bella's reality, for *making* her see me and accept that I exist, has taken a toll on me, not to mention the fact that I barely slept the day before as it is.

I can see her paranoia growing every time she

catches sight of me in the reflections of the glass on the classroom doors, or on the well-polished school floors. Every flinch, every whimper, every tear is another dagger in my heart because this is all *my* doing, but I need to make sure she doesn't forget me.

The moment she decides I'm not real is the moment I'm done for. I can haunt her dreams as much as I like, but she will convince herself that I don't exist, and then I won't be able to plead my case for my family. What good will I be to them then? If I can't get the Chosen One on my side, they will never be free.

I promise you, Bella. Once you understand, I'll make it right. I think to myself, clinging to that ray of hope.

Stumbling down the road, I grunt as I collide with something.

Panic hits me like a ton of bricks, and all the fatigue I'd been feeling vanishes in a second as the fear of discovery replaces it. My skin prickles, and my heart feels as though it's beating on a knife's edge as I hold my breath, waiting for whoever I'd bumped into to recognize what I am and finally turn against me. All because I'm too tired to keep my eyes open and stay alert.

"Uhm, sorry," the something says in a bleary tone.

Raising a brow, I blink at the man who's spoken and cannot help but smile. My fear washes away instantly, replaced by relief and a sense that I cannot *believe* my good luck. The second my blurry vision clears, I see who it is. Bella's older brother, Ash.

"Not a problem," I reply, smiling slightly.

"Hey, I don't suppose you know a good place to have a quick...," Ash makes a sign with his fingers and lifts his hand to his lips in a manner I don't understand, "somewhere private?" he asks.

"I guess? I know a place. If you don't mind walking a bit," I reply back.

In the back of my mind, I ask myself if it's wise, inviting this human back to the place that's become my sanctuary, but at the same time, I wonder if this might be just the opportunity I need to get into Bella's life elsewhere, to get to know her better. Honestly, at this point, anything can help.

"Hey, dude, as long as I can smoke without my parents on my back, I don't care." Ash snorts. "You new here, too?" he asks.

"Err, yeah," I answer him, eyeing Ash carefully as I lead the way toward the outskirts of town and along the canal toward my mountain cave.

"Nice. You know, it's not that bad here. Most people just mind their own business, ya know? I'm just sick to death of this incessant rain!" Ash continues, his voice dreamy and content.

I can't believe how calm he is around me, like the

man in the pub who keeps feeding me for free. Whatever he needs to smoke has clearly blinded him to my true form. That, or he just doesn't care. One or the other.

"I'm Ash, by the way. Ash Nova," he introduces himself, offering me his hand to shake. "Nice to make your acquaintance." He says it in such a posh tone, giggling and snorting in amusement at himself.

I can't help but grin in return, laughing softly as I take his hand and shake it. "Draven Asmodeus. Nice to meet you. Are you Bella Nova's brother?" I dare to ask.

"Ah, are you the one dating my sister?" he asks, eyes narrowing at me.

"No, that's someone else," I reply, unable to keep the hint of sadness from my voice.

"Oh, but you'd like to." Ash grins, handing over the small rolled up wad in his hand that's giving off the most disgusting smell.

"Yeah, you could say that." I laugh, taking the thing from him and following what he had been doing, lifting it to my lips and inhaling it. I cough, and Ash laughs.

"First timer?"

"Yeah." I cough, banging my fist on my chest.

"You'll get used to it." He chuckles, taking it back from me and taking a deep inhale on it. "Stick with me, kid. I'll teach you all that I know." He grins, patting me on my shoulder.

I grin back. I think I'm going to like being friends with Ash.

CHAPTER 6

Spending the day with Ash was exactly what I needed, and I know I have an ally here at the very least. Something about that bolsters me, knowing that I'm not fully alone anymore, that there's someone here I can turn to. I knew I'd been feeling lonely, but I hadn't realized just how heavy the weight of that had been until now.

Smoking whatever he had given me helped me sleep better than I have in what feels like ages. My mind feels free, and my heart is beating so slowly that I keep having to check that it hasn't stopped entirely as I escort Ash back to his house. He's more out of it than I am, so I didn't trust him not to walk out in front of one of those moving contraptions, or drown himself in the canal.

I wave goodbye to him and watch him go into the building before sneaking back into Bella's room, disappointed to find it empty for the first time since I've been contacting her.

Regardless, I slip into the room and lie down on her bed. Breathing it in slowly, relishing in the scent of her and moaning as I imagine her next to me. Closing my eyes, I focus all of my energy on her.

"Bella, Bella Nova." I call to her in her dream, strong and powerful as I drag her back to me.

I stand before her, exposed and alone, my eyes pleading as I look at her while she begs me to leave her alone. I can't. I mustn't. For the sake of my family, I *need* her.

"Bella, please, listen to me. I need your help. My family needs your help!" I plead, reaching out to her, only for her to be dragged into the waking world again. I won't leave, not this time. I'm not leaving until she listens to me.

I stay in her room, hiding in the shadows and out of the corner of her eye, but always close enough as she dresses up for *him*. I hate it. I want to go downstairs and rip his throat open with my nails, but I know I have to wait. I have to make her see. I watch out of her window as they drive away, feeling my heart ache as she vanishes from sight with him once again.

Draven! Please, we need you. They're killing us, Draven!

I wince and shake my head as my sister's panicked dream voice wiggles its way back into my mind. I haven't spoken to my family in days, not daring to reach out to them and admit that I still haven't been able to get Bella on my side, to admit that I'm still struggling to get her to *see* me. My mother would be understanding, but I can already hear the panic in her voice without even speaking to her.

The fear that I will fail, that I won't be able to free them as I had promised. It's not just her fear. It's my own, and as I sit in Bella's room surrounded by the darkness, I wonder if I was ever strong enough for this task.

Why couldn't it have been my sister? She might still be unable to fully control her powers, but she has more strength than *any* of us, and her own brand of chaos might just have been what we needed for this mission.

Asmodeus will kill me if I fail, if the humans don't, anyway. I know that I've been lucky so far, not to be caught by any of them who *might* know what I am. My biggest worry is that he will hurt my mother and sister because he cannot hurt me. I know the demons born in Hell are far more dangerous, and they all want to be free from the Underworld even more than my own people do. I want to be the one to free all of them, to show them that I'm much stronger than they thought I was.

No! I'm letting the despair take over again, letting my paranoia and fear rule me. I've come this far. I can, and I *will*, get Bella to see me for me. I know it. And I'm going to make her help us!

Just as I fix my resolve, I hear the door to the house slam, and footsteps race upstairs. For a moment, I wonder if it's Ash coming back home for another smoke, but I think he's now using my cave as his base for that. I know the parents are out, which just leaves…

"Bella." Her name flickers off my tongue before I even think about it, and I pull myself to my full height, one hand on the wall of her bedroom as though I can reach out and comfort the tears from here. Each sob wrenching at my heart as I want to tear apart the ones who have hurt her like this.

I watch quietly as she comes back into her room,

climbing into her bed and turning off the infernal device for once, the boy's name finally cut off as she does so. So, he's finally hurt her enough, hasn't he? I hate that she's had to be betrayed for me to finally find my way into her heart, but I can't wait anymore. I *need* her.

"Bella Nova, save me," I whisper, stepping out of the darkness toward her.

She whimpers in return, pulling her blanket over her head and sobbing. "Please, not you."

"Bella. I'm sorry. I truly am, but I cannot afford to waste any more time. I need you." I add softly, kneeling on the floor beside her bed. "Not just my family, but me. *I* need you." There's a soft growl in my voice to reiterate my need, and I hate it. I don't want to frighten her in any way.

"Just leave me alone! I can't help you. I can't even help myself. Every time I let people in, I just get hurt, and I... I can't do it anymore!"

"Did he hurt you?" I growl, resting a hand on the edge of her bed, my nails digging into the mattress as my skin prickles with electricity, and my heart swells with anger. The thought of that human doing anything to upset Bella angers me.

"I... I... no."

I sigh heavily, getting up off the floor so that I can

sit at the edge of her bed. I see her pull down her blanket a little so that she can stare at me, her eyes wandering over my body. I can see her fear melt away a little at the sight of my muscles, and I smile softly at her.

"I'm sorry. My appearance can be... frightening," I say softly.

"It... you're fine. Who are you?"

"I told you. My name is Draven Asmodeus, and I need your help."

"You said you needed help for you and your family?"

"That's right, but right now, that doesn't matter. All that matters to me is *you*." I smile at her.

"Why me? Why won't you just leave me alone?"

"Because you're special, Bella, in more ways than I can count. I was sent here by my family because you're the only one who can help us, but I never expected to..."

"To what?" Bella asks, sitting up and staring at me closely, clearly intrigued.

"To fall for you," I admit, smiling again as I see her blush and look away.

"Flattery isn't going to make me want to help you more," she mutters.

I laugh and shake my head. "I mean it. From the

moment I saw you, down by the canal, out in the rain alone."

"You've been following me since then?!" she snaps.

I flinch and look away. "You couldn't see me... because you weren't ready to. It seems that humans have forgotten about us and can't really see me for what I am."

"A demon?"

I nod and rub my face with my hands, my shoulders shaking as I both laugh and cry as she utters the word. I know what I am. I know what I've become, but that doesn't make it any easier to hear when coming from her. I don't want her to see me like this, but what choice do I really have? Without her, I will never be able to go back to who I was, and *this* is all I will ever be.

"Yes. You couldn't see me, either. Not at first; not until I used your dreams. And I'm sorry for that. I know I hurt you, and I know I made you feel like you were going insane, but I had to make you see me so we could talk. That, and... well, I wanted you to see *me*, like I can see you." I reach over and brush a strand of hair back from her face. I know it's a bold move, but at this point, what do I really have to lose?

She doesn't flinch or back away from me. In fact, she closes her eyes and leans into my simple movement, and I smile in return, grateful that she isn't entirely terrified of me. I can see that she's frightened, but that's more due to the unknown rather than *me*.

"I know you've heard it a hundred times before, Bella, and I know you don't know me, but I've watched you from the moment I escaped from my nightmare, and I've been captivated by you ever since. I know you, better than you know yourself, because I've been able to live in your dreams and see what even *you* don't want to admit to."

"Do you have any idea how much of an invasion of my privacy that is?!" Bella cries, throwing the covers from herself and stumbling from the bed and into the middle of the room, her eyes watering as tears begin to run down her cheeks. "Like, it's bad enough that I can't trust the people I *thought* loved me, and now you're telling me you've been stalking me *and* forcing yourself into my dreams without my permission?!"

"Bella, I know, and I'm sorry. I really am, but I don't have the luxury of being nice about all of this," I reply, getting up and following her across the room, my hands on her shoulders as I look down at her. "My family doesn't have that much time, not when they'll be forced to wait *another* thousand years before we can even *think* about stepping foot onto the surface of this Earth. When I was sent to find the Chosen One, I never imagined she'd be this beautiful girl who I'd fall in love with."

Bella gasps at my words, and I flinch. It's all coming out wrong, but I have to make her understand. "You love me?" she mutters, reaching out to touch my arm, her fingers like a flame on my skin.

I jump at her touch, the place where her fingers linger on my skin tingling as though I've been electrified. For the first time in five millennia, I feel like I'm alive, and I can't help but become aroused, thinking about how it would feel to have her hands explore the rest of my body.

I should be ashamed of myself. I know I should, but I'm lost in how I feel about her. My heart swells painfully whenever I think of Bella, and being able to talk to her now?

Without thinking, I grab her wrist and pull her into my embrace, holding her close to me. My breath catches in my throat, and I growl gently, nothing like the sound a predator might make when hunting its prey. It's softer, more sexual, hungry as though I'm struggling not to devour her. I want to, not for food, but I want to taste her.

"Oh!" She giggles, and I blush.

"I-I'm sorry." I move to step away, realizing that she can probably feel me against her, but her fingers grasp at my shirt, and she holds me close. "Bella...," I whisper.

"How do I know I can trust you? Daven said he loves me, said I could trust him, and then…"

"Whatever happened, Bella, do you honestly believe that he didn't know what was going on? I heard you come back crying. I don't know what went on, but I know this. If you had been *my* girl, and I'd seen you upset, then *nothing* in this world would have stopped me from chasing after you. Or banging down the door in order to find you and make it all better. If he truly wanted to make you believe he knew nothing, why is he not here?" I ask.

It was a genuine question. I really didn't understand why he hadn't come to her home if he *truly* loves her the way I love her. I gasp as Bella's fingers trace my stomach, as if reassuring herself that I'm actually real.

"I know you don't really know me, Bella, but I have *never* lied to you. Not once, and I never will. I know my methods have been a bit… rough, but I didn't know how else to approach you, and without you being able to see me in reality, I had no hope of contacting you. And you're our only hope, *my* only hope, not just to save my family, but to save me," I whisper, desperate for her to accept me for who I am and see that I mean everything I'm saying to her. "I will never lie to you, Bella. I mean that. You see me as I am now, at my worst, and if you stay with me, I will prove to you that I mean it. That I'm being truly honest with you."

Her fingers brush against my cheek, and I look down into her eyes, those deep green pools that I could stare into for *hours* without ever getting bored. I want her more than I can ever explain, but how do I show her?

"Do you want me?" she asks, shocking me.

"Yes, I thought that was *somewhat* obvious," I reply, a bit confused. "But I don't want to rush you, either. I know all about your dreams, remember? I know your life because of your nightmares, because of your innermost thoughts, and I... I don't want to push you into something that you're not ready for. No matter *how much* I want you, and how often I've dreamt about you." I growl.

She presses her body against mine, and I hold her close, lifting her chin gently with a finger as I lean down to her. I can feel her breath upon my skin, and I shiver in anticipation, my nerves on fire as I finally relent and press my lips to hers. She tastes even sweeter than I had imagined, but kissing her only makes me want her more, if that's even possible.

Breaking the kiss, I gasp for breath, my hands trembling on Bella's back as I keep her close. "I'm sorry. I just couldn't help myself."

"It's fine, really. I actually enjoyed it." She smiles back at me, her hand resting on my chest and over my racing heart. "I think I need this as much as you do."

A sharp pain stabs me in my heart, and part of me wonders if she's only using me to get back at *him* for upsetting her, but another part of me wonders if I should even care if that's why she wants me. All I've wanted since I first saw her is to hold her like this, to show her how *I* can make her feel good.

Growling low in my throat, I pick her up in my muscular arms and gently carry her to her bed. I hear the sharp inhale of breath, the shock at my strength evident, but she's still not afraid of me. I lay her down and smile at her as she wraps her legs around my waist, making my heart leap into my throat. This girl will be the death of me, in the best way possible.

I slide one hand under her garment, sighing happily as she groans with pleasure as my fingers caress her naked breast, my free hand tracing a line up her inner thigh.

My wildest dreams can't remotely compare to the reality of her breathy moans down my ear, and there's no way I can deny how hard she makes me, not when I'm pressing against her wet bottoms as I lie on top of her. I bury my face into her neck and breathe her in. If this is the only chance I get to be with her, then I'm going to savor every luscious second of it.

I feel her weight shift beneath me, her hands clawing at my back as I touch her through her bottoms, unable to stop myself, whimpering as I feel how wet she is, but I'm still conscious of not wanting to push her too far too fast.

"Are you sure?" I growl softly, looking down into her eyes, my heart hers for the rest of my long existence. "Because once I take you, I'm not sure I'll be able to stop myself."

"I'm sure; make me yours," she whispers, but it's hard to ignore the tears in her eyes.

Removing my hand from her garment, I wipe the tears from Bella's cheeks with my thumb and smile at her. "No man should ever make you cry, Bella. Never. No man is ever worth your tears."

I want her, but I want to prove to her that I'm not him. If I'm ever going to have her heart, then I need her to see that I'm different from the others, from all those boys who *just* want to be inside her for their own pleasurable needs and gains rather than for Bella's.

I roll off her and see the look of shock on her face, mingling with rejection. I can imagine that it's not often a man has ever stopped halfway through sex with her, but I'm not going to be like any of them; I want her for her. Lying next to her, I pull Bella against me, pressing her head gently against my chest so she can hear my racing heartbeat.

"It's okay. I can wait. I've waited five millennia for you. What's a day, a week, a month?" I smile down at her and kiss her head gently.

"You mean that... don't you?" she mutters into my chest, her tears soaking my body as she clings to me tightly.

"I do. As much as I want you, I don't want to push you into it. I know you're thinking about him. I don't want my first time to be about him and not me."

"Your first time?!" Bella gasps, pushing me away gently to stare at me incredulously. "You mean..."

If my ashen black skin could blush, I would have been bright red at what I'd just stupidly admitted to, but I promised Bella that I'd be honest with her, and that's the reality of it. I never took a woman before our banishment; we were far more religious about such things when I'd been human. There were tussles in the hay, little touches here and there, but most of us didn't have sex for the fear of getting pregnant before marriage. We'd never have lived it down, been outcasts in our homes because of it, so it only happened on rare occasions... or for me, not at all.

"I've never been with anyone before. Ever. You would be my first, but I want you to be mine when *you* want to be mine. Not out of anger at someone else."

"Daven," she utters his name as though she just remembered that he exists. "I should call him back." She reaches over and grabs her phone, clutching it to her chest as her thumb hangs over one of the buttons, clearly debating whether or not to call him like she had just said.

Her words are like a knife to my heart. I've bared my soul to her, been honest and restrained myself, as difficult as that has been given how all I want is to feel her wrapped around me.

"Can you trust what he'll say if you do?" I ask, unable to keep my contempt for him from my voice.

She turns and smiles, snorting at my obvious jealousy. "No. Not really... I know he'll tell me that he didn't know anything about it, that he had nothing to do with it, but how can I trust if he's going to tell me the truth? When I told him I was seeing you, he took me to a doctor. He clearly thinks I'm as crazy and insane as those bitches at school think I am. Otherwise, why would he have left me alone *just* as they targeted me with that... box of stuff." She scowls at the phone and tosses it to one side, curling back into my arms. "You're right... I can't trust him. I can't trust any of them. You're the only one who has ever been truly honest with me." Then she takes a deep breath and sighs. "Draven?"

"Yes, Bella?"

"Will you stay here with me tonight?" she asks so quietly that I almost don't hear her.

"Bella, I would like nothing more than that." I

smile, kissing her forehead and breathing her in as I pull her closer.

The sound of her breathing grows softer as she drifts to sleep, and it soothes me. And it's also hard to fight my own exhaustion. The day has been a roller coaster, but in that moment, I'm content with the woman of my dreams wrapped up in my arms.

CHAPTER 7

"Bella! Bella, darling, are you up yet?" Her mother's voice calls up to us, waking us both up with a jolt.

"Oh my god! Can you hide?" Bella hisses.

"Not easily, though chances are, she may ignore me entirely. Though, she may see me as a weird-looking human... I can go out the window?" I grin.

"No, I'm not having you crawl out my window.

Just... stay here a minute. Let me get rid of her. I still have some questions I want to ask you. If that's okay?" she asks, putting a brush through her hair after she pulls on the same garment from last night.

"You can ask me whatever you want. I'll wait here, and if it looks like someone's coming in, I'll go out the window, but not until I'm sure someone who isn't you is coming in." I smile.

"Thank you," Bella whispers, throwing her arms around me and standing on her toes to kiss me.

"Bella?" her mother calls again.

"I'm up!" Bella snaps back.

"Oh, good. Daven's here. He wants to see you."

Bella freezes, her hand on the handle of her bedroom door at the mention of his name. She begins to tremble, her fingers white as she grips the handle tightly.

I hate him. I hate him for ever having the chance to hurt her the way he has, just like all the other men in her life. None of them have deserved her. Not one of them.

"Bella. Go see him if you need to. I can wait here for you or come back later," I whisper to her, placing a hand on her shoulder to reassure her.

"No. I want you to stay. I want *you*, not him," she says angrily, turning her head to kiss my fingers before turning back to the door. "I don't want to see him, Mom. Tell him to go away!"

"Oh... okay. I'm sorry, Daven. She says she doesn't want to see you." Her mother's muffled voice drifts up to us as Bella stands by the door, listening in.

"Bella? Bella, please! Just let me talk to you; let me explain!" Daven calls up to her.

"No! I don't want to hear what you have to say. Just go and see your slut, Stephanie, and leave me alone!" Bella snaps, throwing herself into my arms and hugging me tightly.

I pull her close, unable to keep myself from grinning as she chooses me over that buffoon. Her breathing is labored as her hands cling to my back. Her body presses close to mine, her breasts a hard lump against my body.

"Bella...," I warn her gently, feeling the sudden arousal against my bottoms.

"I want you. I want *you*. I want someone who isn't going to lie to me, who's going to respect me. I want someone who *sees* me." She snarls, her fingers running along my stomach and making me moan in anticipation, desperate for more. "*You* see me. You've always seen me, haven't you? From the minute you found me sitting in the rain by the canal, sneaking your way into my dreams and seeing the worst parts of my life... yet you're still here, and you still love me. I want you. I want *you*, Draven."

It's all I need to hear, and it's the permission I required to let myself go. The growl that leaves my throat frightens me with its lust-filled ferocity as I pin her against the wall, my hand holding her wrists above her head as I nibble at her neck. I had promised to make her mine, and now she's going to be.

She writhes and moans at my touch, wiggling to free herself so that she can touch me in return. Freeing her, we hurriedly take off each other's clothes, and I groan at the sight of her. She's even more beautiful than I could ever have imagined.

The bed is forgotten. I hold her up against the wall and slide inside her with a whimper, feeling her hot and wet parts against me. If I were ever to touch Heaven, this is it, here with Bella in my arms, lost in this sensational pleasure.

When we finish, we collapse onto her bed in each other's arms, panting heavily. I run my finger along her wrist, my eyes drawn to the handprint, *my* handprint, on her arm. "I'm sorry. I never realized I would mark you when I grabbed you."

"It's alright; it doesn't hurt. I suppose I'm marked as yours, better than a ring." Bella laughs. "It's clearly fate. That reminds me, you keep saying that I'm the Chosen One, and that I'm the only one who can help save your family. What do you mean?" she asks, shifting around so she can sit on my lap, wrapping her legs around my back, and making me shudder as her naked breasts brush against my chest.

"You keep that up, and I'm going to be unable to answer." I growl teasingly, running my fingers through her hair. "My family and I, we weren't always demons. Once, we were humans, natives to this land who lived peacefully amongst the other humans who also lived here. Only, the peace didn't last."

I sigh heavily, leaning back against her wall as I ready myself to tell the story of my life. I've never uttered the words aloud to anyone before; it was always my father who reached out to coax the Chosen One onto our side... until he died, and the role fell onto my shoulders instead.

"My family, my tribe, we were deemed evil by some of the other humans. Though I think it was just jealousy and greed. They wanted our land, but we wouldn't give it up, so they called us evil and said we didn't belong. I was young and reckless, and I was sick of my people being bullied and butchered by the other natives, so I stood up to them. The problem was, I stood up to the wrong person."

"What do you mean?" Bella asks, scowling at me.

"I decided to go after one of the other humans who was against us. I stole her livestock and destroyed her crops, like they had done to us, and I mouthed off at her. What I *didn't* know was that the woman I'd targeted was a witch. Because I was young and reckless, I doomed my family, my entire tribe of people, my entire generation, into the abyss of Hell." I croak as the words force themselves from the back of my throat. I know what I'd done was wrong, but I'd never been given the chance to redeem myself.

"She cast us into the abyss, doomed to live in the Underworld with the demons. Some of my people got eaten the minute we arrived. Others, like myself, got turned into demons as well. But we still lived in fear of the others, that they might turn against us at any minute and kill us like the others. Our human souls were trapped in an amulet of yellow and purple, which is why this whole fucking town wears those colors; it helps to keep the spell intact, keep it strong."

"But you got out? How?" she asks.

"Every thousand years, we get the chance to come to the surface. It's said that the Chosen One is the *only* one who can help us be free again. I know it's a lot to ask. I know it's a lot to put on you, but without you, my family is stuck in that pit of fire for another thousand years, in that searing void until the next time the surface opens again, and we can be set free. The portal closed early this time. I was meant to come through with my family, but I was the only one who got out."

"You're alone...," Bella whispers, her hand on my cheek.

"I am, and without you, I'll always be alone. Without you, Bella, I'll never die. I'll never free my family from the Underworld, and I'll never be human again. All because I made a mistake when I was younger."

"And they never gave you a chance to say you're sorry?" Bella asks, her tone growing angry, not at me, but at those who had thrown me into Hell in the first place.

"No. I've had a long time to reflect on my actions. I could have lived with *myself* being thrown into the abyss as punishment, but my family never deserved any of this. None of us deserved the curse that the witch put on us. They started the war against us. All I did was stand up for my people, and they cast us into Hell."

I can see Bella thinking it all over, and I wonder what she thinks about it. I'd had millennia to be angry, to hate humans, to want to see them suffer as we suffered, but this is all still new to her. I'm putting a lot of pressure on her, since my entire tribe is relying on her help to break the curse.

"You didn't do anything wrong, though. None of you. How could they act like you're evil when they were the ones pressuring you in the first place? This was your home, and they took it from you!" she yells angrily.

I nod. I hadn't realized how comforting it would be to tell someone our story, to hear someone agree that our punishment didn't fit our crime, even my own.

"And this entire town is in on it! All of them!" Bella snaps, her hands balled into fists. "Draven, I'll help you. I'll do whatever it takes to free your family and get your human souls back. None of you deserves this. I bet Daven knows all about this as well... I thought I could trust him, but he and his family have all made sure that none of you could live the lives you should have. I promise you, Draven. Whatever I can do to help, I will," she says firmly, placing her hands on my face and staring into my eyes.

I smile at her, hugging her tightly and kissing her hard. "Bella, thank you so much. I love you, and my family is in your debt." I gasp, kissing her again, smiling as she kisses me back.

Mom, Melanesia. You'll be free soon. The Chosen One is on our side now. You're coming home.

UNLEASHING HELL BOOK TWO

LOVING HER

VIOLA TEMPEST

CPSIA information can be obtained
at www.ICGtesting.com
Printed in the USA
BVHW040914260622
640608BV00003BA/28

9 781952 716805